To All the Wonderful Students at the Columbia Explorers Academy!

Have Fun reading, your Buddy Greg.

"08"

A Big Beaked, Big Bellied Bird Named Bill

Written and illustrated by

Greg Watkins

PELICAN PUBLISHING COMPANY
Gretna 2006

I want to thank God for all He has given me, the talent to write and draw, and for the gifts of my beautiful wife, Shanna, and my children, Tracy, Myles, Brianna, and Bridget. I love you with all my heart and soul.

First edition, 2005
First Pelican edition, 2006

ISBN-13: 978-1-58980-441-8
LCCN 2004112590

Printed in Singapore
Published by Pelican Publishing Company, Inc.
1000 Burmaster Street, Gretna, Louisiana 70053

WELCOME
TO
BIRD BLUFF

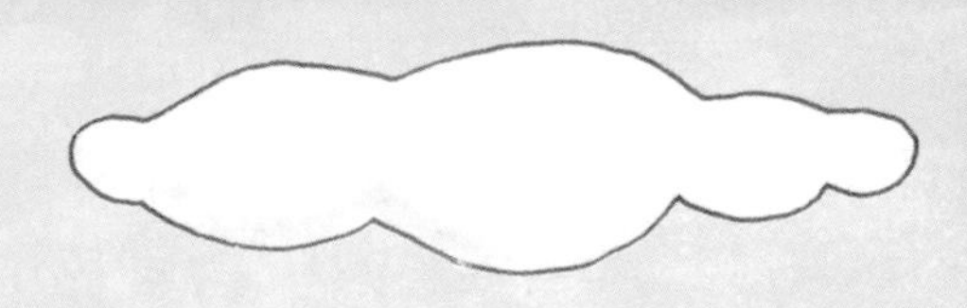

Bill, the Big Beaked, Big Bellied Bird, needed some bird friends. Bill was new in Bird Bluff, and he was shy.

He was so lonely that he decided to risk the danger of big hungry cats and go out for a walk.

As Bill was exploring, he heard birds in the bushes — just what he was trying to find! He hoped they would see him and invite him to join the fun, but they did not.

So Bill decided to be courageous...

"Hi!" said Bill, the Big Beaked, Big Bellied Bird.

All the birds just laughed.

"We don't allow Big Beaked, Big Bellied Birds around our bunch!" said Big Bully Bird.

"Yeah!" said the other birds.

"This is a club for Bird Bluff birds. So... **Beat it!**"

Bill did just that. He ran back into the woods.
Bill ran until he could run no more.
Then he sat down on a log and sobbed...

"Why doesn't a big cat just come along
and gobble me up?!" he cried.

"Hello Big Beaked, Big Bellied Bird," said a worm.

Bill opened his eyes and the worm spoke again.

"My name is Bartholomew, Bartholomew Worm. What's yours?"

"I'm Bill, the Big Beaked, Big Bellied Bird," said Bill.

"What seems to be the trouble, Bill?" Bartholomew asked.

"Well, the problem is that I'm a Big Beaked, Big Bellied Bird, and I'm new in Bird Bluff, and I have no friends, and I tried to meet some birds, but they laughed at me because I look different.

"That's my **trouble!**"

"Well, why don't you come with me to meet my friends," said Bartholomew.

"Okay," said Bill. "But they won't like me either. They'll laugh and make fun of me, just like everyone else."

"I'm not laughing," said Bartholomew. "So we'll just see about that."

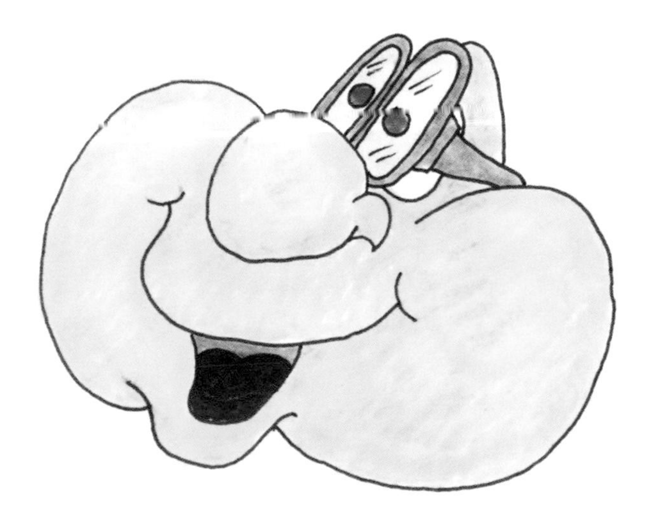

When Bill and Bartholomew reached a clearing, they found Bartholomew's friends.

"Hi everybody! We have a new friend — Bill, the Big Beaked, Big Bellied Bird. Bill, meet DJ Dog, Brendon Mouse, and Bob Cat."

"Hi Bill! We're pleased to meet you."

Bill was puzzled.

"What's **wrong**, Bill?" asked Bartholomew.

"You are all friends? A worm, a mouse, a dog, and a cat? I was always told I should stick to my own kind. You are all different. Shouldn't you be enemies?"

"That's plain nonsense!" said Brendon Mouse.

"Sure, we're all different, but we all **like** each other."

"Sure," said Bob Cat. "That's what makes us special — and interesting."

"You're right!" said Bill.
"I should be **proud**
to be a Big Beaked, Big Bellied Bird.

I'm sure glad I met friends like you."

"Yep!" added DJ Dog. "Being different doesn't make you bad, it makes you an **individual.**"

Back at the Bad Bird Bunch clubhouse, the radio was blasting.

The birds were dreaming up trouble. "Let's go make fun of somebody," yelled Big Bully Bird.

"Yeah," yelled the others, and as they were leaving, a **news flash** came over the radio.

"Today a bird-eating alligator escaped from the Bird Bluff Zoo. All birds should be on the lookout. Now, back to the music."

"Big deal," said the Bad Bird Bunch. "We aren't afraid of any dumb old alligator."

"Yeah," said Big Bully Bird. "Maybe he'll eat that Big Beaked, Big Bellied Bird."

The bunch roared with laughter.

In fact, they were so busy laughing that they didn't hear the bird-eating alligator crashing through the bushes until he was upon them.

"It's the **alligator!**" they screamed.

The alligator backed the Bad Bird Bunch against a tree. Big Bully Bird's knees were shaking.

"Wait Mister Alligator! Don't eat us! Let's make a deal!" he begged.

"Let's hear it," said the alligator. "But it better be good because I'm **hungry!**"

"If we bring you a Big Beaked,
Big Bellied Bird, would you spare us?"
asked Big Bully Bird.

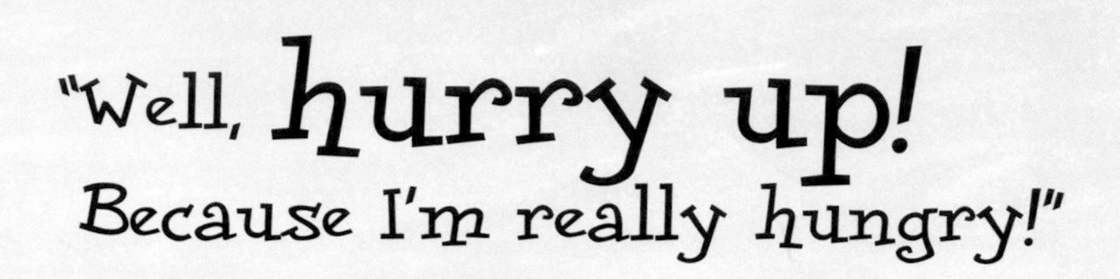

"Blue Bird!" yelled Big Bully Bird.
"Go find *that* Big Beaked,
Big Bellied Bird and bring him
back here – *fast!*"

Blue Bird found Bill a short while later alone in the clearing.

"Bill," he called out. "I thought I'd find you here. We were just teasing you. It was all in good fun. Come back and join our bird bunch club. We really want you to join, but you have to come with me now."

"I don't know," said Bill. "I promised my new friends I'd do some chores while I wait for them to come back."

"Aw, come on," said Blue Bird. "You can even be the first one to walk into our new clubhouse. If you join our club, you won't have to do any dumb work. You should hang around your own kind anyway."

"I don't think so," said Bill.

"Just for a few minutes," said Blue Bird.

"Check out the clubhouse, and then you can leave. You'll be back before your friends even know you left."

"Oh, all right," said Bill. "I guess that would be okay."

When they reached the clubhouse, the Bad Bird Bunch welcomed Bill like a friend.

"Just go into the clubhouse and it will be all over," said Big Bully Bird.

"What do you mean?" asked Bill.

"Nothing," said Big Bully Bird, laughing.

"There's something fishy about this," said Bill. "I don't think I want to go in after all."

At that, the Bad Bird Bunch pushed Bill into the new clubhouse, which just happened to be the mouth of the alligator.

With a **slam** the alligator shut his mouth.

Bartholomew, DJ Dog, Brendon Mouse, and Bob Cat knew something was wrong as soon as they returned to the clearing.

"Footprints!" yelled DJ

The friends followed the tracks as fast as they could to the Bad Bird Bunch.

"Where's Bill?" DJ demanded.

The birds just laughed.

Bob Cat grabbed Big Bully Bird and asked, "Where's our **friend?!**"

Big Bully Bird slowly pointed toward the alligator.

Brendon Mouse bravely ran right over and **bit** the bird-eating alligator on his tail.

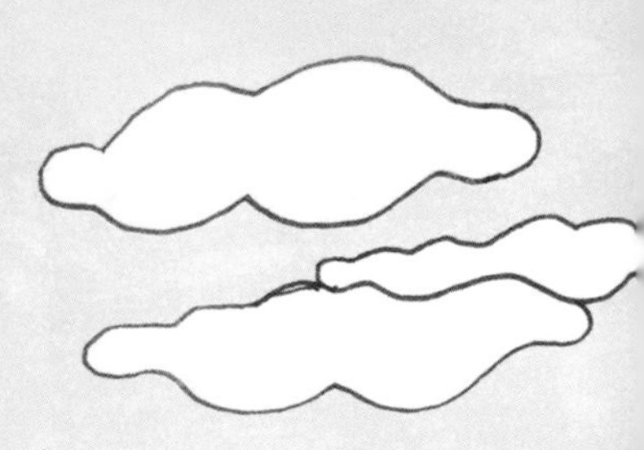

The alligator's mouth opened with a **howl** and out flew Bill.

"Let's go!" shouted Bob Cat, and the animals escaped with their new friend Bill.

"You didn't keep your deal," the alligator roared to the Bad Bird Bunch.

"It's **dinner time**, birds!" he yelled, chasing after them.

At the clearing Bill said, "I'm glad to have friends like you. You saved my life!

"Until today I didn't know a bird, a worm, a dog, a cat, and a mouse could be friends.

"If everyone could spend more time making **friends** than enemies, we could all live happily ever after."

"You're right, Bill," cheered Brendon Mouse. "But there's one more thing we should do."

"What's that?" asked Bartholomew Worm.

"We have to **help** the Bad Bird Bunch get away from that hungry old alligator!"

The End?

What will happen to the Bad Bird Bunch?

Get ready for Book Two...

Brendon Mouse's Big Idea to Save the Bad Bird Bunch

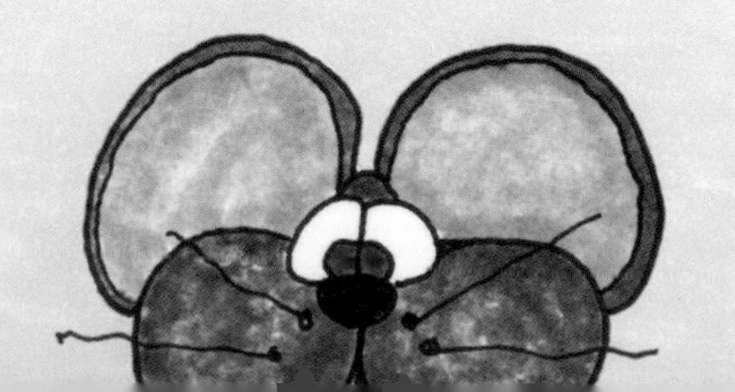